Reading Together at Home

One, Two, Flea!

First U.S edition 1998

ISBN 0-7636-0534-4

6 8 10 9 7 5

Printed in Hong Kong

Candlewick Press
2067 Massachusetts Avenue
Cambridge, Massachusetts 02140

One, Two, Flea!

Allan Ahlberg

illustrated by
Colin McNaughton

DISCOVERY TOYS CANDLEWICK PRESS

One, Two, Flea!

One, two, three,
Mother finds a flea,
puts it in the teapot
to make a cup of tea.

The flea jumps out,
Mother gives a shout,
in comes Father
with his shirt hanging out.

Four, five, six,
Father's in a fix,

wants to get the billy goat
to hatch a few chicks.

The chicks hatch out,
Father gives a shout,

in comes Granny
with her hair sticking out.

Seven, eight, nine,
Granny's doing fine,
scrubs all the children
and pins them on the line.

The line gives way,
Granny shouts, "Hey!"
"Wow!" shout the children . . .

and they all run away.

Tiny Tim

I have a little brother,
his name is Tiny Tim,
I put him in the bathtub
to teach him how to swim.

He drinks up all the water,
he eats up all the soap,
he goes to bed
with a bubble in his throat.

In comes the doctor,
in comes the nurse,

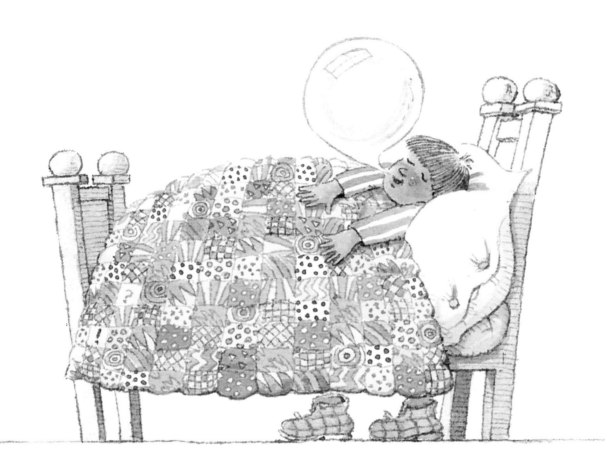

in comes the lady
with the alligator purse.

"Dead!" says the doctor.
"Dead!" says the nurse.
"Dead!" says the lady
with the alligator purse.

But he isn't!

POP!

I have a little sister,
her name is Lorelei,
I push her up the chimney
to teach her how to fly.

She runs across the rooftops,
she chases all the crows,
she goes to bed
with a feather up her nose.

In comes the doctor,
in comes the nurse,

in comes the lady
with the alligator purse.

"Dead!" says the doctor.
"Dead!" says the nurse.
"Dead!" says the lady
with the alligator purse.

But she isn't!

Read it again

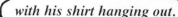

In comes Father . . .

with his shirt hanging out.

Skipping rhymes

These skipping rhymes are remembered in many different versions. The whole family can share their memories. They can be written down and illustrated in a child's book of rhymes — and, of course, skipped to!

Take turns

You can take turns reading the lines of "One, Two, Flea!" See how fast you can read through it.

One, two, three,

Mother finds a flea . . .

In comes the doctor,

in comes the nurse . . .

Act it out

"Tiny Tim" is ideal for acting out, using different voices for each character. It's a very good way to learn the rhyme too.

Groan!

Playing doctors and nurses

Children enjoy playing doctors and nurses. Very few props are needed: a teddy bear or parent with a bad knee, strips of cloth for bandages, and a "doctor's bag" of assorted boxes and tubes for imaginary injections, medicines, and treatments.

Family tree

The same family features in "One, Two, Flea!" and "Tiny Tim." Can you find them? You could try tracing your family tree, including as many generations as possible.

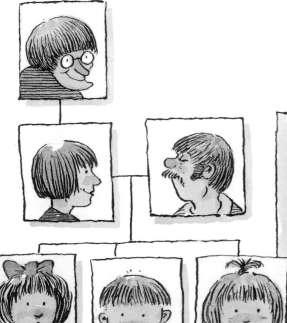

Family rhymes

Reading these humorous rhymes is a good way to begin making up rhymes about members of your own family. You could use names or individual "talents" as a starting point.

My sister Molly
Had a dolly called Polly.
She fell down a drain
And was never seen again.

Reading and Writing

If you and your child have enjoyed reading this book together, you may also enjoy writing about it together. Shared writing, like shared reading, is a wonderful way to help develop children's early literacy skills. Encourage children to write or draw their own version of the story, their feelings toward the story, or an experience from their life that relates to the story in some way. You may wish to paste their work on these two pages as a keepsake and a record of their literacy development. Children not yet ready to write may enjoy dictating a story for you to write down for them. For more information and ideas about writing and reading with your child, please see the *Reading Together at Home Parents' Handbook.*

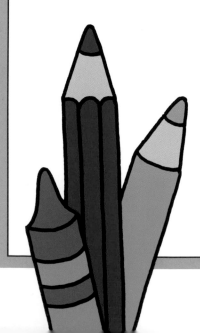

Reading Together at Home

Green Level: Taking Off

How this book helps support your child's reading development:

Children will love the humor in these zany skipping rhymes. Having two of them in one book introduces children to the idea of chapters, especially as the same family is illustrated in both rhymes. The verses' very strong rhythm and rhyme make it easy for children to remember them, so they will be eager to join in the reading. Having some words in speech bubbles shows children a different way of writing direct speech. "One, Two, Flea!" is also a counting rhyme that reinforces beginning counting skills. "Tiny Tim" provides the same basic story in two different versions, so children will feel very confident in predicting what is going to happen next. It is particularly good for acting out, which helps children to feel more involved with the story.

See the *Reading Together at Home Parents' Handbook* for more information on specific reading skills your child is developing as he or she reads books in the Taking Off level of the *Reading Together at Home* series.